Magic Eater

Shadow Hearts Book 1

Shi Elvanian

InExhaustible Media

Magic Eater

Shadow Hearts Book 1

Written by Shi Elvanian

Marketed and Supported by Ruth R.

Copyright 2025

Cover by InExhaustible Media

InExhaustible Media

Thomasboro, Il

10 9 8 7 6 5 4 3 2 1

This book is dedicated to my creative familiar, my cat Jasmine. My feline bestie.
I've also dedicated it to my real life bestie, and my heart Jason.
These words were woven together for those who enjoy the slow burn love story that ends in fireworks of fairytales.

ONE

A Presence

Lyra felt someone watching her. The familiar tingle in her fingertips warned her of danger, despite actively stocking shelves at the bookstore she worked in. As she shelved a worn copy of another classic tome the tingling ran up her arm, making even the fine hair on her neck stand on end.

Experience told her not to turn around. The more obvious reactions often lead to drastic situations no one needs to encounter. Lyra extended her magic out like a wave, reaching for the source in the most subtle manner. The old bookstore held it's own magic which only resonated with her own helping her reach out. As the old brick walls began pulsing with an unfamiliar energy, she realized something felt different.

This presence didn't feel like a threat. It felt curious, maybe? The strange feeling remained difficult to define. A knot formed in her stomach.

Lyra tucked a strand of dark curls behind her ear, using the gesture to glance casually over her shoulder. Through a pile of books waiting to be shelved, she noted a slight shimmer to the air, like a magical impression left behind by an entity or user of magic. Often resembling the heatwaves rising from the summer pavement, she knew others wouldn't note what she did.

"Lyra! Could you please help with register two?" Sarah, the manager dear to her heart got her attention from the front of the store. "The card reader's acting up again."

"Coming!" Lyra felt grateful for the excuse to move, but knew the line must have backed up. As she moved away, she pressed her hand against the shelves, leaving a trace of protective magic, as her grandmother taught her. If anyone with poor intentions were to cross the barrier, she'd know.

The shift passed without further incident. The lingering sensation of being watched never fully left, but the pressing nature from early in the day diminished and distracted less. By close, her shoulders ached from the persistent tension and vigilance. Walking to the break room the sunset painted the floors in warm fall hues.

"You okay?" Sarah paused their steps to face Lyra.

"Just tired." Lyra forced a smile. "Midterms and projects." This wasn't the time to share her magical affinity or the fact she felt a confusing energy in the store all day.

Sarah nodded. "I remember how tough that period is. If you need a hand with anything, let me know. If you ever just need a quiet place, the store is always available. You've got a key."

Lyra smiled. "Thanks. I try not to stress on it, but I will keep the quiet escape in mind."

The pair made their way out the front door and onto the street. As Sarah locked the doors, Lyra realized the feeling of being watched disappeared. She exhaled, smiled, and they split ways.

Lyra started the three block walk to her apartment. It was only a block and a half before she started feeling the odd energy again. Tingling came with footsteps. They were back. Her hair on her arms stood again, but she didn't turn.

Lyra slipped her hand into the pocket of her pants, wrapping her hand around an enchanted rock her grandmother gifted her years before. The stone warmed as she ran her thumb over it, preparing to release the stored magic, if needed.

"I wouldn't do that, if I were you." The male voice startled her, despite it having some element of comfort to it.

Without sparing a moment, she spun around, extending her arm with the glowing stone between them.

The man stood there, hands raised with his palms open. He was tall, with pale blue eyes that seemed to catch what little light extended over the horizon. While he skin was pale, it wasn't unnaturally so. Despite this, the way he held himself indicated something other than human.

He continued, "What is coming will not be affected by the protection spell."

"Who are you? Why are you following me?" Lyra tightened her grasp on the stone.

"My name is Adrian. I am following you, but someone else is hunting you." He didn't move, keeping his hands up in surrender. "Someone far more dangerous than me."

She saw nothing to indicate he was lying, but more clearly needed shared. "What do you mean by hunting me? Who are they? Why me?"

"I don't know their name, yet. They've been tracking and hunting people like us for months now. Maybe longer." He paused briefly before adding, "Those of us with abilities that aren't known by the common world around us."

"What exactly are you?"

A wry smile lifted the corners of his mouth exposing teeth a little too sharp to be human. "That is complicated. I'd be happy to share more with you, once we are somewhere safe."

"A vampire," Lyra breathed the words. Her grandmother mentioned the creatures a few times in her life, but always as something to avoid. This felt different. He stood with fading daylight shining on him.

"That is an oversimplification, but close enough." Adrian glanced over his shoulder, more alert. "We don't have much time. They're coming."

Cold washed over her, a creeping sensation entirely different from Adrian's. It felt wrong, twisted, spreading around them like oil across clear water. Despite not changing her focus on the stone, it grew cold in her hand and the glow disappeared.

Her instincts screamed whatever was coming was far worse than the possible vampire ahead of her.

"Right now, we don't have much time." Adrian moved closer, his voice lowering to just above a whisper. "The thing hunting feeds on magic. You are practically radiating it. I can help you hide it, even teach you to mask it if you want. But we need to move, now." He dropped his hands and extended one towards her. "Let's go."

The cold sensation felt stronger and Lyra's usual barriers recoiled. Her usual pulse in the world around her shook instead before stopping completely. Her eyes dropped to his extended hand, then lifted over his shoulder as shadows behind him seemed to move with a mind of their own, against the wind, as if tendrils of darkness reached for them.

Lyra took Adrian's hand.

In an instant, his cool hand clutched hers and began moving swiftly down a few blocks from where they were. Within moments they began sprinting through alleys and side streets. As Adrian pulled her into a steady run, she found her lungs began to burn. He showed no indication of slowing, and the twisted cold sensation continued to follow, despite his taking them in seemingly random directions.

Just when Lyra thought she couldn't go any further, Adrian pulled her into a narrow doorway and pressed them both out of the street as far as he could. As he covered her body with his he muttered something in a language she didn't recognize. The air around them thickened, not just in the way it felt, but even physically changing near them. As she glanced over his shoulder, holding her breath, she noted how everything beyond the doorway looked like it was covered by a layer of frosted glass.

"Concealment," he quietly explained. "Not as elegant as your type of magic, but effective, ancient."

Lyra wanted to ask about how he meant 'her type of magic'. In her experience, only her grandmother sensed energy the way she could. Adrian stood here, different, yet familiar with it. Her breath caught when she saw it.

A figure passed through the alley, passing the doorway they stood in. Unnatural grace enveloped this twisted, nearly human shaped shadow. As it passed, Lyra's magic seemed to move away from her in a way she never experienced before. Silent. Untouchable. Unnatural.

Neither one of them breathed until the figure moved on again and the cold sensation faded behind them. As it did, another whisper came from Adrian in the unknown language. The air around them lightened. As she moved out of the doorway, she realized her fingers were intertwined with Adrian's. She pulled her hands together, rubbing her palms with her thumbs in the process. "What was that?"

"I've been trying to figure that out. It showed up in the city about a year ago. It started as something that felt off, but not threatening. That changed when people with magic or an affinity for magic began disappearing." He took a deep breath before he continued, "You're the first person I've found that might be strong enough to help me stop it."

Lyra leaned against the wall, mind racing. She glanced in the direction the shadow form went. Her magic remained beyond her reach. In the space of an hour she went from student and bookstore clerk to enchanter capable of facing a magic eating shadow creature. Stopping that shadow creature was beyond anything she accomplished thus far. "What makes you think I can help?"

"I've been tracking this on some level from the beginning. When the first magical beings disappeared, I started trying to locate, warn, or protect them."

"Ah, so you're not a vampire. You're a guardian angel." Lyra folded her arms across her chest.

Adrian closed his eyes briefly before continuing. "Those I watched over from the shadows, never noted I was there. Those I introduced myself to, didn't connect why I was invested in their safety until I explained myself. You are the first, and thus far, the only person who identified my energy. From what I saw, you identified the energies in the walls of the bookstore as well. You even connected the underlying vamperic elements without running." He slightly smiled. "At least not until I wanted you to."

She couldn't explain it if asked, but she smiled when he did. This burden he spoke of felt too heavy for one person to shoulder. It would take time to process. She knew nothing about the vamperic classes or even magic. Things appeared like change on the horizon. "What's next?"

"Now," Adrian began, "we figure out why that thing is hunting people like us. Then we'll figure out how to stop it before it gets stronger." His blue eyes met her warm brown eyes. "First, we need to teach you to hide your magic better. Right now, when you are relaxed, you are like a beacon to that thing right now. You are a natural magic user. You seem to be connected to the environment in a way many others are not. Because of that, you touch so much with the slightest hint of magic no matter what you are doing. We need you to be like this," he gestured to her. "controlled, contained magic that can't be seen oozing into the world around us."

Lyra's hand slipped back into her pocket, wrapping her grandmother's cool stone in her hand again. "You can teach me?"

Adrian nodded. "I can."

Lyra considered her previous experience with other magic users. Most were passing sensations in crowded places. The fleeting sparks of recognition often disappeared before she could narrow down the source. Once, in her freshman year of college, she spotted a woman in the library whose hands sparkled with a frost as she turned pages. Lyra tried to approach her, but the woman disappeared among the stacks before she could.

Another time she identified the unmistakable pulse of healing magic from an elderly man on the bus. His arthritic hands glowed faintly as he massaged his own wrists. Their eyes met and he nodded a silent acknowledgment, but shook his head when she moved to say something. Lyra knew these people differed from her and with this information she wondered how these people were doing.

Often her grandmother explained magic users kept to themselves for good reason. "Power recognizes power," she'd say, "but that's not always a blessing." Standing here with Adrian, Lyra began to understand what she meant.

"Okay." She nodded and sighed. "Teach me."

Two

Foundations

ADRIAN LED LYRA THROUGH a maze of ever narrowing streets, deep in the old side of town, and far from the grid of downtown she comfortably knew. As they moved the last glints of sun light sank into the horizon. The night surrounded them, silently reminding her not to reach out to the world around her. The October winds brought a fall breeze, causing her to rub her arms, and pull her jacket closer. Adrian remained unbothered by the temperature or wind.

After following in silence for several minutes, Lyra asked, "Where are we going?"

"Some place safe. Some place your magic will not the be the beacon to the shadow."

She continued to follow him for several minutes more before she realized they stood on the roads near the docks. "It's cold."

"The wind from the river can be chilly this time of year."

He continued forward until they were in the warehouse district beyond the docks. "I have a workshop in an old, warded building. It's an ancient magic that will prevent the hunting creature from sensing us."

She nodded as he spoke and within moments she noticed they stepped onto a street filled with industrial sized warehouses. Many appeared to be repurposed. Some of the transformed buildings were lit up with strings of colored lights, while others featured murals created with spraypaint. Half hung 'No Trespassing' signs, faded next to broken windows in yet unchanged buildings.

The building Adrian stepped in front of held nothing of the sort. The solid brick building stood taller than many, indicating multiple floors to this vast structure. Nothing tattered the walls, or decorated the brick. "It's not as bad inside."

He pulled an ancient-looking key from his pocket. The ornate key slid in effortlessly, and the click resonated off the walls nearby.

A chill ran down her spine.

Stepping over the threshold opened into a vast open space. Above were exposed beams. The walls, while far apart, seemed to segregate different areas. One section held a vast collection of maps, some clearly antique. Many of the maps held colored pins and connecting threads between the pins. Another area filled with ceiling to floor bookshelves. Many book covers were simple, possibly recovered, or ancient.

Closer to the door on a large vintage carpet a sectional leather sofa decorated the space with end tables and a coffee table stacked with open books, notepads, and magazines. "Your workshop?"

Adrian nodded, placing his keys on a nearby wooden ledge. "Among other things."

Lyra wandered through front room. Her fingertips traced over the closest shelf, feeling the smooth wood. Along the sides of the bookshelf she noticed symbols carved into the frame. As she traced each one her finger tips tingled slightly.

"You can feel it, can't you?" Adrian watched from behind a desk as she explored. When Lyra looked at him, he added, "The ancient history in these walls. My family lived on this land, and eventually in this building for generations. Long before this city was founded, the first protective wards were placed here." His voice softened to a tone of reverence. "My great grandfather carved the symbols you're touching. My grandmother added her own in places too. This building, this home, is more of a legacy filled with magic and stories."

"I can feel that." Lyra turned around as her magic finally relaxed outward touching the walls, and the ground. "It's layered. Deep. Kind of similar to tree rings. Perhaps each generation added a protection or ward of their own."

"Ancient families are complex." He gestured to the nearest couch. "Please, sit down. I think we have a bit to discuss."

"I have a question first." Lyra crossed around the back of the couch and settled within a few steps of where he gestured. "Why do these wards feel so different?"

"There are many different kinds of wards, magic in general. One is Blood Magic. That's what you're feeling here. You often use a natural magic. Many people like you are scantly aware of it in existence, or that they can manipulate it at all. Many people do not realize they are like us, actually use this natural, passive kind of magic. "

"I remember my grandmother mentioning that to me."

"Good. Are you aware of other magic forms? Light manipulation? Dark Magic? Necromancy? Water manipulation?"

"I've never seen any of it, but I know of them." Her brown knit. "Grandmother often spoke about much of that. Right now, I wish I listened more."

Adrian shifts to a seat across from Lyra. "The blood-bound wards are an ancient type of magic, far older than most. It's far less flexible than your magic, or most others really, but it is permanent or at least the closest thing to it we have today." He placed his elbows on his knees. "Understanding what these are is easier than using each of the types of magic without time and practice and where possible, a teacher."

"Right." She paused, trying to form the thought into a sentence took longer than desired. "You said there were others like me? Others who were hunted?"

The change in Adrian's expression hinted at the darkness of the creature they encountered. He stood and walked to a wall of maps not far off. Touching the first red pin, he explained, "Anna Chen was the first to disappear. She sang to plants, encouraging them to grow. Her magic seemed as passive as your interactions with ancient energy in the environment. Initially, I wasn't sure she even knew she could use the magic with intent. I watched her for a few weeks to see if she would do something that seemed to catch attention of our creature. The creature, until that point, only drained some a bit, but never killed. Anna was the cross over I never hoped to see."

Lyra's lips pressed into a thin line as he spoke.

"David Klein, hardly eighteen when he began speaking to spirits freely." He sighed. "I watched from afar as he spoke to the spirit of a woman before the creature showed up. The woman turned to the creature and then disappeared as particles within seconds. David, on the other hand, aged rapidly right in front of me." He wiped his hand over his face. "I was too far away. I couldn't stop it."

"Sara Okafor interacted with threads of probability, even nudging them on occasion. She went to work one afternoon, and didn't make it home. I got there in time to see the creature withdrawing from the alley near her job." His eyes dropped to the ground. "Marcus Rivera could manipulate metal with his thoughts. He used that to defend himself when the creature arrived. I wasn't too far away that time, but I wasn't much help either. I tried to warn him, but Marcus didn't realize his skills were magic and didn't believe me." He took a deep breath. "I did what I could to protect him, but by now this creature, this shadow, got much stronger. My wards barely slowed it down. My knowledge and access to magical energy is not enough alone. Nothing Marcus did even slowed it. I don't think it even touched him this time to drain him. I thought for sure I was next. Instead it kept going. The only thing I can think is that my magic doesn't meet the needs of the shadow being."

"You keep saying that your magic is different. How is it different?" Lyra leaned forward on her knees.

"Magic like you know it is natural. It's like breathing, or blood flowing. Those like me borrow that. Our power, our magic, is transformed, much like we are. I can sense magical beings, but I can't perform more than a few basic spells or wards. Each one simpler than the last. While it is effective, it is not strong. I can learn more unique skills, but it's not a thing that could stop that shadow alone."

He stood and moved to a cabinet next to the bookshelves. "The first thing we need you to learn is how to draw your magic inward." Adrian picked up a candle and hand held mirror. "Think of it like closing your hand around the flame. You won't put it out with your hand, but you can limit its reach." He placed the items on the coffee table between the seats. "It's truly beautiful to those who can see it, yet dangerous in our current situation."

"How will these help?" Lyra gestured to the mirror and candle.

"The candle will help you visualize." Adrian's smile caught her off guard. It felt infectious and she smiled despite not knowing what he was about to explain. "The mirror is just a mirror. The catch with it though is it has been treated to reflect magical energy rather than just the person gazing in it. You will see what I see when I look at you."

Lyra felt heat in her cheeks. "Okay. How do we start?"

Over the next hour, Adrian guided Lyra through exercises. Each exercise provided insights Lyra hadn't learned as a child. She saw her own magical signature in the ancient mirror, a swirling aurora of gold and green that wrapped around her like a second skin. She noticed the relaxed waves of light that drifted from her skin with each relaxed breath. With Adrian's patient instruction she pulled her light closer to herself. When she noticed the light shimmered instead of expanded, she knew the process worked.

"Good." Adrian's silk voice commented after several minutes of her holding the aura tight against her. "Let it breathe. Holding it too tight can be a different problem. Think of it like a cloak, not armor."

Lyra relaxed control slightly. The mirror showed her energy pulse with her breath. "How did you learn all of this? I thought you said you couldn't preform this magic."

"I've spent a long time observing." Adrian paused. "While I can't perform magic, I see how it works. Sometimes the outside perspective is more valuable. Also, magic intertwined in my life in various ways from birth. I don't get the same feeling about magic from you."

"You were born, not changed?" Lyra tilted her head.

"That is a different story." He crossed the room to the nearest window. "It's late. Even if you don't feel exhausted yet, it won't be long." His gaze returned to her. "You'll need to practice regularly until you can conceal yourself well enough not to trigger our hunter."

Lyra longed for the comfort of her own place. She wanted the time to process everything. She also didn't know how much she could trust her new teacher, although nothing about this evening caused her magic to warn her. Instead it felt comfortable in this environment. Magic never misled her. "Do you have a spare bedroom?"

Surprise flickered over Adrian's features. "You'd trust me, this place enough to truly rest here?"

"My magic does and it is never wrong."

He nodded. "There is a room upstairs. It has separate wards and the doors lock from the inside." He started across the room. Lyra followed.

They ascended an iron spiral staircase to the second floor. Lyra found herself studying his movements as her grandmother's warnings about his kind echoed in her thoughts. He moved with an inhuman grace, but emitted a gentleness in all he did. He was not the predator her grandmother swore all vampires were. She wondered how long protecting magic users from the shadows led his steps.

The guest room, while small, held heavy drapes and a plush bed. Across the room was a window with a seat and bookshelf filled from floor to ceiling right next to it. She turned and true to his word, the door held a line of serious looking locks. The wards humming in the room were different than the ones that protected the whole house.

"Thank you." Her hand rested against the doorway. "For warning me and teaching me."

"I appreciate that you trusted me when I did." A slight smile quirked at the corners of his lips. "We will figure out our next steps tomorrow. Hopefully, I'll have some kind of sense of these patterns before getting rest myself. Tomorrow, it would be good to work on maintaining shields while using your magic. It's one thing to hide it while sitting still…"

"…and another to hide it in the real world." Lyra nodded as she finished the sentence. "I look forward to learning."

He turned to leave but before returning down the stairs he added, "Whatever happens from here, whatever you learn, don't let fear of that shadow creature make you afraid of your own power. Your magic, a natural living magic, is rare and precious. No one and nothing should make you dim your light."

He descended the stairs, leaving Lyra to consider his words as she prepared to rest in the guest room. This was easily the strangest ending to what started as a perfectly normal weekday.

THREE

Revelations

MORNING LIGHT FILTERED THROUGH the thin space between the drapes of the guest room's window. Lyra felt momentarily disoriented by the unfamiliar room, until the events of the previous evening flood back to her. Her protective stone rested against her chest, warm and soothing.

After swinging her legs over the side of the bed, she considered the lessons she practiced the night before. Carefully she ran the exercises through her mind again, trying to repeat each one at least once before getting moving for the day. The smell of coffee urged her downstairs.

Following the scent down the old iron spiral staircase led her to the kitchen in the corner of the vast room downstairs. Adrian stood over a stove, dressed in black jeans and a soft color sweater, stirring something in a pot.

"You cook?" Lyra caught the surprise in her tone with a moment of instant regret.

He glanced over his shoulder. "I may not need to eat as often as you do, but yes, I cook." He nodded towards the mug of coffee on the counter. "That's just poured, black. If you want cream, it's in the fridge."

Lyra reached for the coffee. As she wrapped her hands around the warm mug, the moment of normalcy shattered as reality came to mind. "I should call work, and my professors." She took a deep sip, noting his nod. "I can't exactly tell them I'm taking time off for magical self defense training."

"Stomach flu is always reliable." Adrian suggested as he plated eggs, toast, and some ham for them both. "Highly contagious, and no one asks too many questions." His expression met her level of serious. "We need at least a few days to train you. While the exercises and lessons aren't hard, they do require focus and muscle memory."

"Right." She took a bite of the ham first. "Mmm." Her eyes drifted up to his gaze. "You're good."

"Thank you." A tint of red to his face caught Lyra's attention. "You should taste my souffle."

"Looking forward to it. And I think I want to try to share some bit of truth with the teachers, and really my boss. She's aware of my gut instinct on things and really appreciates it. I think I might be able to explain that I've got something else going on that requires me for a bit. How long I guess we'll have to figure that out, right?"

"I don't know how long training will go. Some people catch on quickly. At some point, I am sure you'll have to get back to your usual life. Speak to your people as you believe you need to or can."

Lyra nodded, and considered suggestions with a deep sip of the coffee.

Adrian took a few bites of his breakfast. "We'll get started when you're ready."

Lyra nodded and worked through her food.

A comfortable conversation accompanied the remainder of breakfast. Once they cleaned up after breakfast, Lyra excused herself to make a few calls. Adrian cleared a space in the middle of the room. When Lyra joined him again, he positioned her in the center of an ornate rug.

"First, we need to establish your baseline." He stepped back. "Let your magic flow as naturally as you usually would. I want to see how it moves."

Lyra closed her eyes and let out a deep breath. She opened her barriers and relaxed. Her magic responded eagerly, reaching out to brush against the walls, testing the wards. The waves of magic crashed against the walls like water on the shore. This comfortable relaxed state left an acute awareness of the room around her.

An intense wave of something seemed to be focused on her. She opened her eyes. The hair on her arms stood when she realized the intensity her magic conveyed was evident in Adrian's gaze.

"Extraordinary," he murmured. "Your magic seeks connection. It's rare to see any move so ...alive." He shook his head slightly. "That's exactly what makes you vulnerable to our shadow friend."

He stepped next to her, exhaled, and lifted his hand. She felt a coolness in the air between them. "Can you feel that?" She nodded. "It's like your magic is trying to communicate something with you. He looked at his hand. "Focus, you should be able to see the magic like tendrils wrapping around the fingers."

Her gaze shifted to his hand. She watched as his skin seemed to shimmer. It felt like her magic interacting with whatever ancient blood magic he knew. The sense she got from it was clearly a connection, and not one she ever experienced before.

"Your magic reaches out. Try to pull it back to you. Imagine curling up like an armadillo, wrapping it tight around you."

Lyra tried. For almost an hour after their magic connected, she struggled to contain it. Silently she focused inward, drawing it to her. Every moment she thought she wrapped a tight grasp with it, it slipped free. The connection created with Adrian's magic drew hers to it.

"It feels like holding my breath." Lyra's frustration was evident in her tone.

"You're fighting its nature instead of working with it." He paused. "Try treating it like a river instead. Direct the flow instead of stopping it."

Lyra closed her eyes and tried this new approach. By late morning she found it was possible to create a direction for her magic. Wrapping the pattern around herself from head to toe and back drew it from a magical bonfire to a calming magical glimmer.

"Good." The smile that danced on his lips drew Lyra in for a moment. "Take a break. We'll work on maintaining it after lunch." He moved toward the kitchen again. "You might want to check your phone."

A moment later Lyra cringed at the number of notifications waiting on her. One by one she responded. After responding to her grandmother, she considered adding an update about what they were facing, but chose not to worry her. Next was answering questions from friends and family, and emailing her professors. Once all notifications were sorted, the phone slid back in her pocket.

In the quiet moment, Lyra wandered to the bookshelves. Many books in this area were old, some held lingering traces of magic. Titles ranged from mundane to mysterious. Classic literature sat next to books in languages she couldn't read. Many spines were marked with symbols instead of letters. Her fingers trailed along the shelves while she read until something familiar struck her.

This energy almost sung to her through the magic woven in her being. The book was small, bound in faded green cloth. "The Natural Current: A Study of Living Magic," She read the sticker aloud. Her grandmother once tried to press the book in her hands, warning her she'd need it one day. Teenage Lyra dismissed it. In the years that followed, the old, dusty book was lost.

"Find something interesting?" Adrian's voice startled her. He chuckled.

She turned to look up at him. "I think my grandmother tried to give me that book once." Her gaze returned to the green book on the shelf. "I didn't really read it then."

"Probably good to do now. You can take it." Adrian reached past her to pull the old tome from the shelf. "Grandmothers are often wise about such things. Eliza Blackwood knew more about natural magic then anyone I'm aware of in known magical history."

Warmth from the pages brought a level of comfort reminiscent of summers visiting with her grandmother. She settled in an oversize chair nearby and began reading the book. The book weaves details with application for each nuance of the natural magic she is familiar with. The details expand upon lessons introduced earlier by her grandmother.

The author spoke of magic as a living force. The people with an aptitude for the interaction with this natural magic held the potential of creation within them. This was far beyond anything she experienced, but could see where it was possible with the information contained in this book. The book explained much of this kind of magic required an understanding of nature as it is, and helping it along. This form did not require the give and take of other forms. Life expanded instead of energy traded.

When she came to the chapter title: 'Dark Reflections: The Prices of Severance' her breath caught. "Adrian, you might want to hear this."

Leaning over her shoulder a moment later, she read, "Those who attempt to sever their magic, or another, from the natural connections risk more than failure. Magic, being alive, requires those connections to maintain the bearer's very essence. For a variety of reasons, some have tried to accomplish this. Their fate is uniformly tragic. They are neither dead nor truly alive. They become hollow beings, capable only of consuming magic others wield. The innate, instinctual effort to restore the severed connections push the shell of the being to restore the severed connections. Until they are fully lost, this shadow of the previous being will continue forward to this end."

"Well," Adrian exhaled. "That sounds familiar."

Lyra continued to read. "It says such beings are drawn to magic users not just for power but in an attempt to recreate what they scantly recall when they were whole."

"A magical vampire, in essence." Adrian mused. "Though considerably less charming than the mythical kind."

"If it was once a magic user," Lyra spoke each word slowly, "then it had to have life. A name. A story we should find out-"

"We might find a way to stop it." Adrian straightened. "I need to review my research." Within seconds, he stood in front of his hung maps with renewed purpose. "I need to review the research again. The disappearances might have begun before Anna Chen. If we look back further, search for users who might have attempted severance..."

While he began his search again, Lyra turned back to the book, now hoping to find an answer to their problem. A magic user who tried to change their connection to the natural magic, maybe to make themselves more powerful as they would master another form, maybe for another reason, terrified her. This meant their enemy wasn't a mindless force of destruction. Instead this was a person who made a terrible choice. Someone who now yearned to undo their mistake in the worst possible way.

The following hours ticked by. Each one of them doing their part to find answers. Adrian cross referenced his data with previous records. The shifting of pages on the desk or opening of drawers to find new data occasionally broke the silence. A page turn often followed as she continued reading.

Finally. Something useful. Actionable.

"Adrian, listen to this," Lyra's tone carried a hint of excitement. "The severed beings remain bound by the fundamental laws of the magic they are or were connected to. They can be drawn to objects, places, and even people who held significance in their former life. This connection can form the basis of a containment ritual." She lifts her gaze from the page to the man across the room. "It goes on to describe exactly how to anchor a severed being to the connection from their life. Creating some kind of magical prison to limit their destructive nature."

"Good." He returned his gaze to the notes in front of him. "I think I have something too." He tapped a few things in the search engine again. "Come here. I want to show you this."

Lyra dropped her feet to the ground and moved behind the desk within moments. An answer on the horizon felt like security in a dire situation. As she looked at the monitor the image of a professor and laboratory manager faced her. The image showed a middle aged woman with shorter brown hair half up and down with soft curls. She wore a professional suit, in bright white.

"Meet Eleanor Voss." He scrolled lower. "She studied at MIT, but also sought a degree from Exeter University with a focus on the Occult." Adrian placed a hand on a pile of papers. "If you read these, you'll see she held a theory that Occult magic and witchcraft as it was once known. Eleanor dedicated her studies to identifying the nuances that allowed magic as spoken of in history to stir the results they cataloged. Basically she applied the scientific method to magic, hyperfocusing on results. She married while seeking her double degree. Not long before graduation, her husband fell ill with an aggressive form of Pancreatic Cancer." He took a deep breath and let it out slowly. "They bought a house here in town. She withdrew from her remote attendance courses in the UK, finished her degree at MIT and began teaching at the college here in town."

Lyra stood up again. "So he died then?" She began pacing.

He shook his head. "Not right away. He actually went into remission for a while. She continued to grow in her position and began leading a lab. While in remission, he even finished his degree."

"Okay, they had time to further build their bond and love."

He nodded this time. "And then the cancer came back with a vengeance. It was months from the time they learned they were facing it again and his funeral. Her mother moved in at that time. Eleanor poured herself into work after. It looks a lot like her research was turning from the scientific approach to something more fantastical. If I had to guess, based on a mix of published and unpublished papers, she was looking for reviving the dead."

Lyra paused her steps. "She put that in her papers?"

"Not explicitly, but she did speculate on ways to revive natural cell re-production in unhealthy organs. She also spoke about reinitializing human cellular production postmortem." He spun in the chair to face her. "Nat-urally this was presented in scientific magazines with a focus on medical approaches so she didn't reflect on the magic side, but it wasn't uncommon for her to reference the fact people have sought answers to similar things since the opening of records, even occasionally referencing the historical solutions in magic."

"Presenting her studies as one thing to keep her grants while working on bringing her husband back?"

"That's my guess."

Lyra started chewing on the inside of her lip. "Do you think she was trying to sever her connection to bring him back?"

Adrian shrugged. "Maybe. For someone with that much love and loss, it might be enough to risk everything."

Lyra half nodded while she began pacing again. "How long ago did she ...?"

"She was listed as a missing person a few years ago." Adrian lifted a page from his desk that looked like it came from the newspaper. "There were a few electrical disturbances around her lab for a few weeks before one day it exploded. Her body was never found."

He stretched out a few of the pages in front of him. "Look at the patterns of the disturbances around her disappearance. Compare that to the disturbances I've found around our shadow's movements. It's a similar type of disturbance. Almost like the changes, pops, and flow changes precede the movements." Pulling another stack of pages from the printer he placed them next to the images and charts. "This is her notes on the last experiment they released after her death. Might have just been part of the case. It seems like the changes were expected on some level."

Lyra looked over the documents, trying to make sense of the equations.

"I think she was trying to use science to amplify her magic. Less research into it and more try to do it better."

"And you believe this is what caused her to be severed." Lyra pressed her lips into a fine line while she thought. "Timing seems right though. The book indicated the change isn't instant. It would happen over time until their humanity evaporated." She took a deep breath. "The longer they remain in this state will lead to needing more magic to recover even a hint of who they were. It's instinct, if I am understanding what I read."

"Assuming this is Eleanor Voss, her lab might still be accessible on the campus. It's not uncommon for colleges to preserve places like that for years in situations like this. At least not uncommon at this university."

Lyra glances over to him. "We can bind her, according to the book. We need three things. Something personal to her. Something that meant a lot while she was still herself. To contain her the ritual requires an anchor point that connects with them on a deep personal level."

Adrian already started pulling out boxes, and settled back at the seat a moment later with a photo. He passed it to Lyra and began sorting a few of the papers on his desk. "According to the police report, she was mentioned wearing a pendant all the time. It wasn't found at the lab. Her mother explained the pendant was a family heirloom. Something passed from one family member to the next for generations. She had barely passed it on a few weeks before her disappearance." He glanced at the page in his hand. "They didn't search her home though. This sounds like it would be the exact kind of piece we might want for an anchor."

Lyra glanced at the picture of the pendent. It was distinctive. A silver compass rose, held in a small hand. "It's certainly unique enough. I know I wouldn't be wearing something like that during some kind of ritual or experiment that might go wrong."

"She also had a house near the edge of town. They didn't mention much of an investigation there. More they collected a hair brush and a few other items. That pendent wasn't mentioned at all there either. Even if we don't find that, I'm sure the house will have something that will work as an anchor. What else do you need?"

"A place of significance and a conduit of magic."

"We could check into her lab. And maybe her house will operate in a few ways. What is suggested for a conduit of magic. I'm not sure what I have here that could fill in for that."

"I could be the conduit. Using my magic to bind her to the anchor in her place of power is possible."

"That's extremely dangerous." Adrian shook his head. "You're new to all of this, at least at this level." He sighed and gestured to the walls around them. "This place... my family has always stood between magic users and those who would harm them. I won't break that trust now. And if we don't try, she'll keep hunting, keep consuming, trying to fill a void that can never be filled. You have no such tie."

"We need to try something as soon as we are ready. There are too many lives at stake." She shook her head. "I can't sit still knowing I can do something."

"This just isn't my favorite idea."

"We're doing this together. You've got more experience than I do." She put the photo on the desk. "We'll be fine."

Adrian smiled. "Your confidence is reassuring."

Lyra couldn't help smiling in return. "Well, I guess we have some work then." Her eyes drifted back to the picture. "I am sure this isn't what she wanted. She wanted to change something, improve something. Maybe bring back her husband."

"I will look for the pendent at her lab. You need to master the ritual. The process will need to be exact. Don't rush learning it."

She nodded and handed him back the image.

"Thank you for doing this Lyra. Thank you for not running, like any other sane person would have done. I can only do so much, but with your help this will work."

"My grandmother always told me that some fights find you." She considered her decision and her grandmother. Her mind wandered through the little information they've uncovered on the previous magic users taken, but also to Eleanor Voss and the tragic choice she made. As she settled down to review the containment ritual, she started looking for a way to save both the severed shadow and stop the victims.

Four

Racing Time

NEARLY MIDNIGHT FOUND LYRA fighting frustration. Her movements must be exacting. Hours of practice still didn't lead to the results she needed. Her gestures faltered, and missed sometimes by the littlest amount. She memorized the exact gestures, practiced, and still didn't hit the target.

Adrian placed both of his hands on hers. "You need rest. You've been at this for hours. We both have. We can't do this if you're not at your best." He pressed his index finger on the scowl on her forehead. "You're kind cute when you are upset."

She rolled her eyes and looked away.

"I may have a lead on the pendent. Katherine Voss, Eleanor's mother is living in a care facility in a town nearby. She's currently in a live in care assistant for the facility. Accordingly the facility, has a record of a jewelry cleaning service days before Eleanor's disappearance."

"That's a little personal to be able to get." She side-eyed him as she spoke.

"I have help where I need it." His open palm gestured to the building. "My family connections are in a lot of places. That's neither here nor there.

We have evidence the pendent in question may not have been available to Eleanor on the day she disappeared."

"That's promising."

"My thoughts as well." He released Lyra's hands. "I am going to check out her house, first. If I don't find it, I am going to visit with her mother." His phone audibly vibrates.

"Something important?"

He slips it out of his pocket and looks at the article and video he was linked to. His expression darkened and he turned the phone to face her. The social media feed showed a clip of a young street musician preforming downtown. The headline read:

Popular Downtown Performer Missing. Last Seen Tuesday Night.

In the video the musician played an acoustic guitar with remarkable skill. His fingers moved over the strings like wind tickling the strings. What caught Lyra's attention were the pigeons behind him that seemed to dance in perfect synchronization with the music as it was played. It looked choreographed. The timestamp on the video indicated two days ago. The night she met Adrian.

"He's like us." Her voice was barely above a breath.

"Looking at him, I doubt he even knew it." His eyes dropped to the ground for a moment. "She would have sensed him though."

"That's the night we came here isn't it? That's who she went after when you saved me." She started biting her lower lip.

He nodded. "She found another target. Based on my understanding of things, she'll need to feed again soon. She's consumed a lot of magic, but it wasn't as powerful as yours is. Also, it seems her consumption time has shortened significantly. Like an addiction getting worse."

Despite the warmth in the room, a chill ran down her spine. "How soon?"

"If my observations are accurate and her hunger is accelerating," He pinched the brow bone between his nose. "A couple of days, maybe less if she's desperate enough."

They both watched the video a moment longer, watching the magic influence the birds around him. The display felt beautiful. Unfortunately this marked him for consumption by a shadow entity. There were others, many others. The emotional weight of this loss hung between them.

"I need to get back to practice." She sighed. "The containment ritual is complex. It needs to be perfect."

"We need rest," Adrian finally broke the silence. "Both of us. We won't be able to help others if we too exhausted to think straight. A few hours of sleep should help us tackle this fresh."

Lyra began protesting but a yawn betrayed her. "You're right." Her gaze returned to his eyes. "Even vampires need rest sometimes?" She tried to come across lighter than their situation.

Adrian ran a hand over his face. "After working on this for days, it's a good idea." He half smiled. "Four hours at least."

Lyra nodded, yawned, and stretched. "Maybe stretch it to six?"

Adrian nodded this time. "Six hours is sensible." He smiled. "We can't rush this. We both know this needs to be perfect or it won't hold. Trying to do this exhausted won't help anyone."

She side-eyed him. "What progress have we made? What don't have much time before she strikes again. I don't have this right, despite memorizing the patterns."

"I know her private lab in Pierce Hall hasn't been touched, beyond becoming listed as storage." He pressed his lips together. "At least we've both made some progress."

"There were two labs?" A silent nod between them was all they needed. Lyra yawned again.

"Let's get some sleep."

She agreed with him and made her way back to the guest room she rested in the night before.

Lyra woke with her heart racing, ready to get back to practice. Within minutes she washed and returned to the practice area set up the day before. They might have two days before the shadow takes another life, another magic user, another member of a dwindling population of people. Whoever she picked up on next depended on Lyra to get this right. Failure was not an option.

She continued the ritual, gestures, and movements while maintaining her protective shield. No matter how exact she got the movements, or words, she couldn't maintain the shield. Each attempt, despite only trickling out enough magic to know it worked or not, left her more exhausted than the last.

"Again." She spoke out loud, more to herself than anyone else. Her hands rose to begin the sequence again. Magic responded to her more sluggishly than previously. Her confidence began to fade.

"Your pushing too hard." Adrian's voice broke focus. "The magic needs to flow freely, naturally."

"I know!" She dropped her hands. With a sigh, "I am sorry. When I focus on the containment weave, my shields slip. When I reinforce the shields, I lose the pattern." She dropped into a nearby chair. "I need more time to practice."

"It's not about practice." Adrian spoke quietly. "You're attempting opposing types of magic. Containment requires your magic to reach out, create and weave bonds. The shield is holding it inward, hiding your signature. It's something few can do, and fewer who can do it well."

"How are we supposed to do this?" Her focus remained on her hands. "I can't complete the binding if she attacks."

Adrian remained in pensive thought for several minutes. "There might be another way." He moved swiftly to the bookshelf nearby, pulling leather bound volume with an unmarked spine. "It's something my family has used on and off for generations when normal magic isn't enough, or right for a situation." The book cracked as he opened it. Showing it the greatest care, he placed it on a nearby table, turning each page with reverence. "Blood wards are different than magic protection. As long as a source exists, the wards are self sustaining."

"Blood wards?" Lyra leaned forward, studying the pages in front of him. "Like the ones protecting this building?"

"Similar, yes. These would be temporary, focused specifically on concealing your magical signature during the ritual." He hesitated before continuing. "I can create them. It's something unique to my nature, however, I've never preformed one myself. I've studied it, practiced too, but haven't ever used one like this."

"Eleanor's hunger is growing. I can offer my blood."

"No. You need all of your strength for the containment spell." He pressed his lips together. "I think I can get help from another magic user. She uses a healing specialty at the local hospital." He glanced up at her. "Besides, blood magic is the domain of vampires and their kin. It isn't something a living magic user should be an active part of."

Adrian's phone buzzed actively with several notifications again. As he looked over them his face turned grim, again.

"More bad news?"

He nodded. "I'll handle the blood wards. The nurse at Metropolitan Hospital is a familiar contact."

"You'll just walk up to her and ask for blood?"

"Not exactly," he half smiled before continuing, "but I have a plan. First though, you need to master the containment ritual. Each gesture, every word."

"How long do you think we have?"

"It's been three days, which means she held out longer than I thought she would."

Lyra sighs. "So, she's been fed, again. Another three days?"

"I wouldn't be surprised, but obviously it's possible. I think two."

"Then we get back to work. I'll start on the third sequence again."

Adrian spends the next few hours walking through it with her, helping her where he can. By midnight he's ready to head out. With a promise to Lyra that he'll be back by dawn, he shrugged his jacket on. "Adrian, be careful. We can't have her sense what we are doing."

He glanced at her with a smirk. "Always am. Family tradition and all." A moment later he went into the night.

Lyra continued to practice for a while longer before retiring for the night, still not satisfied with her results. She had less than a day to get this right.

By morning he returned from the Voss house, holding a precious silver compass rose pendant. Holding it she could feel faint traces of magic still locked inside. "This will work," she felt more confident than the night before. "I can still feel tendrils of connection to it." Looking back up at Adrian she added, "Now those blood wards, with this, we can end her hunger."

Adrian nodded and shifted toward the door again. "I'll handle that part. Make sure your ready tonight. Her lab isn't far off, so we will time this right."

They couldn't keep waiting. Tonight they will bring this to an end.

FIVE

Convergence

Pierce Hall loomed against the darkening sky. The Victorian architecture cast elaborate shadows across the empty campus quad. Lyra remained sheltered among the small grove of ancient oaks. She ran her thumb over the stone her grandmother gave her in one hand. In the other hand, she clutched the pendant. Both hummed with a stead magic as if responding to what would come.

Adrian stood in the open, not far from Lyra. His gaze continued to roam the expanse. She knew he wanted to be sure the quad was clear, or clear enough to ensure safety. Earlier he extended blood wards over areas people could be caught to protect possible bystanders.

"Are you ready?" Adrian's voice carried over the distance between them as if he stood next to her.

Lyra noted the blood wards that seemed to shimmer with power across the quad. She took a deep breath and exhaled slowly, centering her thoughts. "Is it possible to ever really be ready?"

"In time."

"I am as ready as I will be." She looked right at him. "How long do you think we will have?" Her eyes began noting the shadows around them.

The ones dancing around the street lights as they began to turn on felt intrusive.

"Not long. We know she's hungry and we know she wants your magic." He looked over his shoulder at her. "As the shadows creep we are opening her to a stronger base. Start the ritual the moment she comes into view, don't hesitate."

They stood on the very ground Eleanor attempted the magic and technology research that led to the situation. Here the containment would be strongest. The anchor would hold and they would be able to protect. The obstacle might be the magical conduit. It is unusual for the person actively engaged in the binding to be the conduit, instead of sourcing one. As a natural wielder though, Lyra knew it would be possible to complete this as the conduit. She also knew her grandmother should never find out.

What lay ahead will mean either saving the others like them, or losing themselves to the darkness.

"Now."

Lyra relaxed and released her magic freely for the first time in days. It poured out, extending itself along the ground, comfortably touching all things with life. The wind blew through the trees as it responded to the expansion of life in the magic. The animals initially seemed to respond calmer, relaxed. As it touched Adrian, it seemed to wrap around him as it used to do for her mother. An odd experience, but the last few days he was her teacher. As the tendrils of life touched the darkness, it continued on, briefly.

The change to the air felt dramatic, rapid, fast. Ambient temperature plummeted. Shadows crept at first, then poured over the boarders of her magic. It poured into their area like spilled ink, spreading smoothly along the surface of the ground. Lyra's magic recoiled, instinctively. She forced herself to continue the display of power.

Adrian put words to her thoughts, "She's coming."

The sense of wrongness approached.

Lyra shuddered.

A figure, wrapped in shadows, emerged. It still had a human like form, but also didn't. Shadows both preceded and followed every movement, as she swiftly crossed from the doors of Pierce Hall. As she slid passed a light source, Lyra noted elegant features hinting beneath the surface of shadow. Twisted by hunger, it was evident by action this was Eleanor Voss, and she was desperate to feed.

Eleanor Voss arrived.

Lyra's fingers closed around the compass rose pendant. While she began the ritual, Adrian began the blood incantation. The words weren't a language Lyra knew. Every tone held weight, substance. The world around them responded like stones being dropped in still water. Within moments a protective barrier rose between them and Eleanor. A faint crimson gathered and shimmered in the dark.

Eleanor's form writhed at the sight of the barrier. Her hands, if you could all it hands, reached out and the blood ward responded, causing the shadow to recoil.

As Lyra completed the first layer of the containment ritual, Eleanor responded in voice. "No. Don't. Stop."

Adrian glanced at Lyra then turned back to Eleanor. "We can't. You need peace."

"Peace. Yes." It sounded like a hissing sound emerging from the shadow with every word. "Help. Feed me."

Lyra shook her head, hands trembling, she moved into the second level of binding, extending the pendant in her outstretched hands.

"Mine!" Eleanor called in the same snake like tones. "Stop."

The sound resonated with Lyra, leaving the feeling of both rage and longing. "You severed that connection. We will help you find peace."

Eleanor threw herself, her shadows against Adrian's blood ward. It held.

"I was close. I learned." Eleanor threw out the shadows again, recoiling again with an indication of pain in her tone. "The foundation. We can do more. It's more." She threw out the shadows again, and her form began to shift, grow. "Taste. I need a taste. I need connection."

It was clear she held some of her memories, or perhaps as she fed the day before, they were near the surface. She proved to be thinking, calculating. Her form continued to shift and her voice hissed, "The vampire! Kill the vampire. He keeps us from the prize."

The writing shadows condensed into the shape of a spear. Tendrils reached out around and below the barrier, impacting Lyra lightly, as her magic flared defensively, changing focus from the second level of the ritual she nearly finished. Cold spread down her arms from the impact to her finger tips.

It was a moment later she glanced over to see the shadow spear impact Adrian directly. The shadow flew threw the barrier, as if it weren't there. The strike threw Adrian back. Despite the impact with the ground, he stood again, quickly. Blood trickled from his nose. He restored the barrier within moments, proving his skills were taxed.

Frost began visibly forming around the impact.

Lyra moved into phase three of the ritual, and Adrian moved to her side. They continued the incatation gestures.

Eleanor lashed out again. She could not force her way through this barrier, at least not yet. Her shadows struck at them, around, below, and from behind. Her command of the darkness made her more dangerous, even as Lyra continued to move through the ritual.

Lyra's fingers became numb, until Adrian placed his hand over hers. Despite the frost extending over his body, their hands together radiated with warmth. Their magic seemed to wrap together.

Eleanor screamed out in pain with every gesture. Her thrashes continued to slam into the pair, drawing blood and amplifying Adrian's powers. As they moved through the last gesture, last movements of third ritual, the scream and the attacks stopped. Silence. Exhaustion. Pain.

The pendant in her hand grew cold. The design now held new etching, runes of sorts, holding the magic eater within its new prison. This connection to her other life held her safely within.

As their knees began to crumble beneath themselves, they both tried to hold each other up. Their magic continued to intertwine.

"Your frozen," Lyra mumbled against his shoulders. Ice touched her face.

"You're bleeding," he countered. His fingers began tracing some of the shadow slashed wounds, gently, despite the seeping blood.

"Is it done? Did we do that?"

"We did." His eyes dropped to the pendant in her now lose hand. "Keep her safe. We can studying the binding. Maybe we will understand what went wrong in her research, so we can ensure it never happens again." He reached for the hand Lyra held the pendant in. "Perhaps, in time, we will be able to help her truly find peace, without consuming others."

Lyra nodded.

They caught their breath.

"Let's go home." The dark frost finally began to recede. Adrian wrapped an arm around her shoulder.

Together they made their way back to his ward covered home.

Each one moved with exhaustion evidently in their gestures. As they did, questions continued to flow.

If different types of magic are incompatible, why did theirs combine? What really caused Eleanor to change? How many lives did she take? What comes next?

Epilogue

As the door swings open, Lyra and Adrian limp in the room. Lyra closed the door and hears, "It's about time you got back." She tenses. The familiar voice shook her.

"Grandma?" She spins.

In the center of the room stood an elegantly dressed woman, wearing a large flashy hat with a flower in it. Her dark complexion almost glowed beneath the lights. "What happened to you?" The older woman gestured to Lyra's arms and face. "Why are you hurt?"

"How did you get in my home?" Adrian barely pushes out.

Grandma waves off his statement with a gesture. "It's not hard. And there's a key under the box, like always."

The older woman moves across the room to meet the two as they enter. Her head shakes looking over Adrian. "How did you get shadow frosted? What did you do to manage that?" Her head looks at her granddaughter. "Why haven't you healed him yet? Oh." She sighs, waves her hand towards Lyra. The wounds on her arms heal, rapidly. "Pick your jaw up off the ground. It's not archaic magic or something." Her focus turns to Adrian. "Shh." Her hand lays flat against his chest and after a moment the frost deep in his body disappears. "What were you two doing?"

As Adrian's strength returned his gaze leveled with the woman in front of him. "How did you know about the key? Who are you?"

"Eloise Kane. I realize you don't know me, but your family does." She looks at Lyra as she continues, "You might know me as the Enchantress Eloise."

Lyra's eyes widen. "You were mentioned in the book."

"Yes, well, that's not important. Who were you fighting?"

Lyra lifts her hand, extending the pendant.

Eloise takes the pendant, and waves her hand towards Adrian when he attempts to move towards her to take it. The man is held still with the gesture. "Tsk, tsk. She actually went through with it."

"You know this? Her?" Adrian's indigent tone made his thoughts on this woman obvious.

"Yes, young man I did. She consulted with me several times. This is Eleanor Voss. Brilliant young woman but not a natural magic wielder. She worked to force it." Her eyes landed on Adrian. "Why is she bound?"

"She threatened lives."

"Was she the shadow? The Magic Eater?"

Lyra nodded. "Yes. It was terrifying."

"There aren't enough magic users here. You must have been an emergency flare to her." Eloise sighed. "You have so much to learn." Her gaze drifted to Adrian. "You too. Where are your elders? Why are they no longer here?"

"How do you know so much about my family?"

"Go read your uncle's records and you'll find out." She took her hat off. "Tell me, do you still have the rune guest room?"

Adrian's brows knit. "Yes. It's dusty, but – wait!"

Before he finished the response, Eloise started to walk in the direction of the room. "I'll see you two in the morning!"